CIP data is available.
Published in the United States 2013 by
Blue Apple Books, 515 Valley Street,
Maplewood, NJ 07040
www.blueapplebooks.com
First Edition 10/13
Printed in China
ISBN: 978-1-60905-351-2

2 4 6 8 10 9 7 5 3 1

Visit Ethan Long at:
www.ethanlong.com

Scribbles and Ink

the CONTEST

by
ETHAN LONG

BLUE APPLE

Chapter 1

THE CONTEST

What is it, Ink?
JUST THE MOST EXCITING THING EVER!

DRAW A DINO! WIN A PRIZE!

Show all your friends how **GREAT** you are!

FIRST PRIZE is a fabulous trip to

MUDSPLASH MOUNTAIN

The **MUDDIEST** place on earth!

DEADLINE: tomorrow.

YUMMY
MUD SICLES
A whole day spent in mud? I can't wait.

I'M GOING TO RIDE IN THE FRONT OF THE MUDSLINGER!!

Gee, Ink, I've never drawn a dinosaur before. They're so big and...
THEN LET'S GET STARTED!

OK, but...
I'VE GOT YOUR PENCIL RIGHT HERE!
YOU GO FIRST!

Chapter 2
SCRIBBLES SCRIBBLES

AMAZING!
TEETH-TASTIC!

THE BEST TAIL EVER!
SO POINTY!

TA-DA!
What do you think, Ink? Will we win the contest?

WELL, IT'S . . .

IT'S KIND OF LIKE A . . .
Like what?

IT'S A CHICK-A-SAURUS!
It is?
BEHOLD ITS BONY THIGHS AND FEATHERY BODY!

sigh.

Chapter 3
INK-SPIRATION!

SCRIBBLES, BUDDY! I WAS JUST MEANING THAT YOUR CHICK . . . I MEAN, DINOSAUR WAS SO AWESOME, SO . . .
DRAW!

STRETCH
ONE . . .
TWO . . .
THREE . . .
CLICK
CLICK

CRUNCH
CRUNCH
CRUNCH

I'm waiting.

HMMM.
A-HA!

Interesting.

BEHOLD!

Wow! That's the coolest egg I've ever seen!

But where's the dinosaur?
THE DINOSAUR IS INSIDE THE EGG!!

Do you really think we can win the contest with this?
UMMM . . .

Chapter 4
EGG-SPLAIN THIS!

YIKES!

MOMMY!

MOMMY!
I AM NOT YOUR MOMMY.

MOMMY?
Nope.
Sorry, dude.

ME CRY, WAAAAAAH!

BOO-HOO!
Should we draw him a blankie?
I HOPE HE DOESN'T POOP.

THUMP
THUMP
THUMP

MOMMY?

My Boo-Boo Baby!

MY MOMMY!

Chapter 5
BEST EVER?

There goes our prize.
YEP.

Are you sad, Ink?
YEP.

NO MUD-TASTIC TIME FOR US.
Nope. Sorry, buddy.

See you later?
I GUESS SO.

HEY, SCRIBBLES, COME HERE!
I HAVE SOMETHING FOR YOU.

I MADE YOU THIS!
Wow! It's the greatest prize EVER!
Best Buddy AWARD
1ST PRIZE
Scribbles

I have something for you, too!
Best Buddy AWARD
1ST PRIZE
Scribbles

YOU'RE GIVING ME BUCKETS?!
The surprise is inside the buckets!
Ready, guys?

MUD PARTY!!!

THIS IS THE BEST IDEA EVER!
SO WHO WINS THE CONTEST?

EVERYONE!
PLOP!
The End.

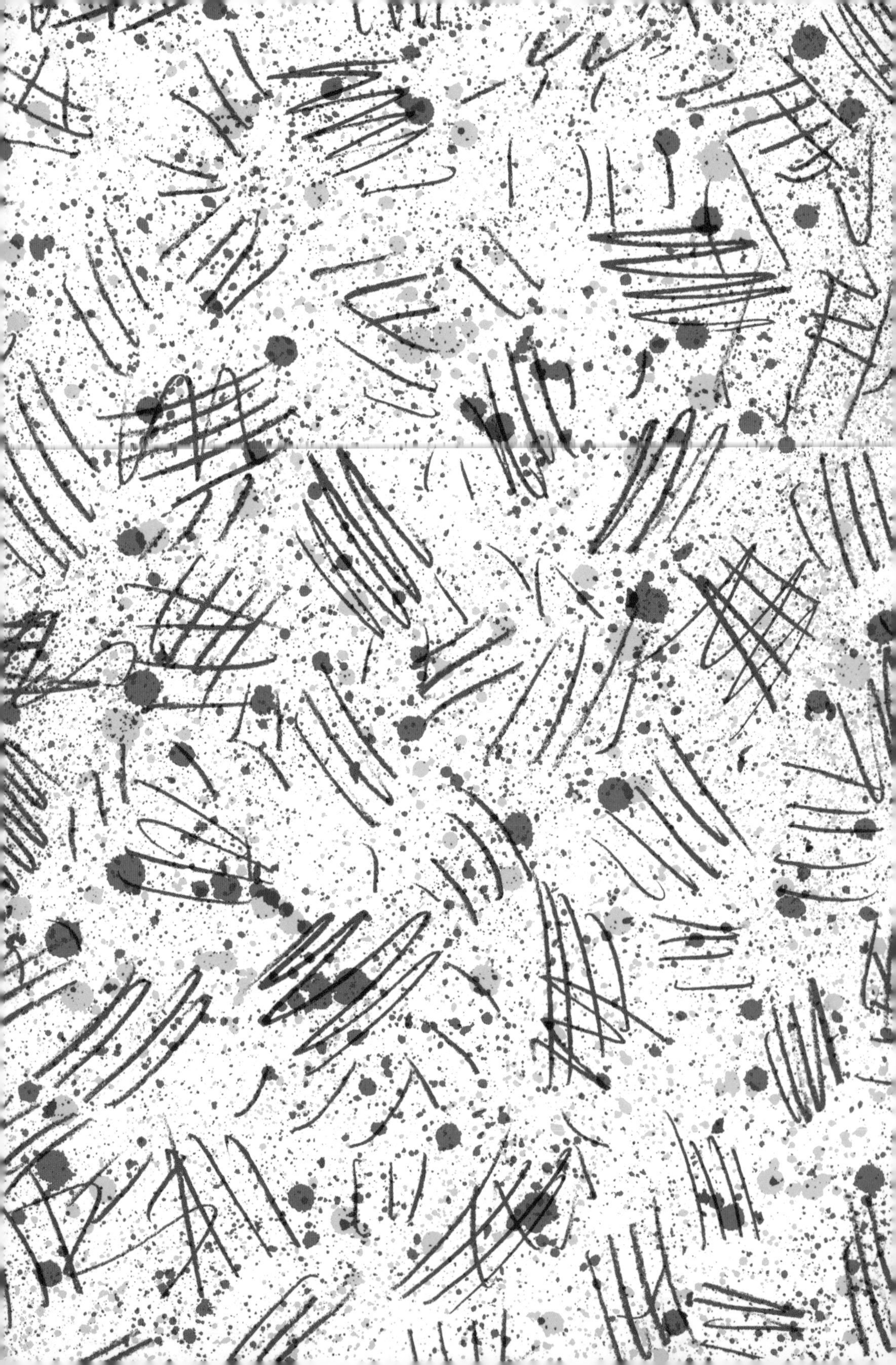